Zoinks! Thirty-eight flavors? Like, am I dreaming?" Shaggy's eyes are huge as he gazes at the colorful sign over the counter. He gives himself a pinch. "Nope, I'm definitely awake. Cool! Now the only thing to decide is where to start." He strokes his chin. "What do you think, Scooby?"

Scooby licks his lips. He doesn't say a word. He just starts pointing at the tubs of ice cream arrayed behind the glass.

"Chocolate praline supreme?" asks the boy at the counter. "Sure!" He scoops up a big mound of that flavor. "Oh, and peach cobbler, too? Excellent choice."

Scooby keeps pointing, and the boy keeps scooping. Finally, he hands over the cone.

Scooby closes his eyes and smiles. "*Ranks*," he says as he begins to lick.

"Great idea, pal," Shaggy says. "I'll have what he's having," he tells the boy.

The boy sighs, rolls up his sleeves, and starts scooping again.

You exchange a look and a smile with Fred, Velma, and Daphne. You've met your friends at the ice cream shop so you can hear about the latest mystery they solved.

Shaggy and Scooby sit down at the table. Both of them carry a towering cone. You check the menu and decide on a strawberry shortcake cone.

"So, tell me about this mystery at the dinosaur museum," you say.

"We went way, way back in time for this one," Velma says. "At least, it felt that way. Those dinosaur bones were the oldest things I ever saw!"

"*Rig rones!*" Scooby says.

"True," Shaggy agrees. "It would take years to bury one of those in the backyard, wouldn't it, Scoob?"

Scooby nods. "*Rou ret,*" he says.

"But it won't take you years to solve this mystery," Velma tells you. "Not if you use our Clue Keeper. I took all the notes this time. Everything you'll need is there, from suspects to clues. Watch for the 👁️👁️, so you'll know who the suspects are. And when you see the 🔦, you'll know you found a clue."

"If you pay attention and take good notes in your own Clue Keeper, you won't have any trouble solving the mystery," Daphne says.

"But, like, you'll need to keep your strength up," Shaggy says. "How about another scoop of ice cream?" He and Scooby have already finished their giant cones. Shaggy rubs his full tummy.

"You two have appetites like Tyrannosaurus Rex," Daphne says, giggling.

Scooby raises his paws, makes a scary face, and gives a huge roar.

"Yikes! Scoobysaurus!" says Shaggy. Everybody laughs.

You finish your cone, wipe your hands, and pick up the Clue Keeper. It's time to check out this prehistoric mystery. You turn to *The Case of the Terrifying Pterodactyl.*

Clue-Keeper Entry 1

"Littletown Museum of Natural History," said Fred, reading the sign over the door of the big granite building we were entering. "This looks like a cool place."

"Like, definitely," Shaggy agreed. "They're even serving breakfast." He pointed to a big banner stretched across the entrance. "Special Exhibit! Pterodactyl Eggs!"

Daphne shook her head. "First of all, that's an exhibit, not a meal. Those eggs wouldn't be too fresh, anyway. And second, it's been canceled." She pointed to a sticker across the banner.

"I think that may have something to do with why we're here," I said. "Professor Peabody, the director, sounded pretty upset when he called me."

"Did I hear my name?" A man emerged from the front door. He was dressed in a safari suit and had a big white beard and mustache. "Welcome to my museum. I'm so

glad you could come." He shook everyone's hand as I introduced the gang. Then he led us into the museum.

"Wow," Shaggy said, looking around at the great hall we'd entered. The floors were marble, and the ceilings were very high. An enormous dinosaur skeleton loomed over us. "This place is awesome."

"But empty," said Professor Peabody, sadly. "I'm glad you like it, but we need more visitors, or we'll have to shut down."

"It seems like lots of people would come to see pterodactyl eggs," said Fred.

"That's what I thought," agreed Professor Peabody. "But I didn't have a chance to find out. The eggs were stolen."

"Stolen?" gasped Daphne. "Who would do such a thing?"

The professor shrugged. "That's what I hope you can figure out."

"What do the eggs look like?" I asked.

"Dr. Sharkey can tell you," the professor said, waving to a man who had just entered the great hall. "He's the curator here, a very esteemed paleontologist. That's a kind of scientist who studies dinosaurs," he added.

Dr. Sharkey nodded to us. "Nice to meet you," he said. He wore a white lab coat, jeans, black-and-white high-top sneakers, and had messy brown hair that looked as if it hadn't been cut — or even combed — in a while. "How can I help you?"

"You can describe those eggs," the professor said. "These kids are going to try to help figure out who stole them."

"Well, well," Dr. Sharkey said. "Good luck to you. The eggs look tan and leathery. They are rock hard since they are fossilized. These are the eggs of a pterodactyl, which is a pterosaur, a flying reptile, not a true dinosaur at all."

"Do they make good omelets?" joked Shaggy. "I'm kind of hungry."

Dr. Sharkey didn't laugh. He didn't even smile. "Those eggs are very valuable for scientific study," he said. "They should never have been treated as a cheap attention-getting device. And I imagine that whoever stole them is far away by now." He nodded to us, turned, and walked away.

"Don't mind Dr. Sharkey," said the professor. "He spends most of his time in the laboratory downstairs, working on his projects. He forgets how to deal with people sometimes, because he practically lives with the dinosaurs." He smiled and rubbed his hands together. "Now! First things first," he said. "How about a tour?"

"Zoinks! Some of these dinosaur skeletons are almost kind of creepy, with their big teeth and huge claws. But, like, this place is cool. I can't wait to look around some more. So, did you notice the 👁👁 in this entry? Cool! That means you've met a suspect. So, like, answer these questions."

1. What is the suspect's name?

2. What does the suspect do for a living?

3. Why would the suspect steal the pterodactyl eggs?

"Like, excellent answers! Let's keep digging for clues so we can solve this mystery before lunch!"

Clue-Keeper Entry 2

"This is the Great Hall," the professor told us, with a sweeping gesture. "Here we have our largest specimen, it's from the Jurassic period."

"Wow! Those are some big bones," I said, gulping as I looked up at the skeleton. It was almost as big as a building!

"We're very proud of it." The professor

smiled at me. "Now, if you'll follow me, I'll show you some of our other dinosaur displays." He led us into another room that was filled with glass cases. Each one contained a display: dinosaur skeletons, dinosaur footprints, and dinosaur eggs. Everything looked very, very old. It was amazing to think that these creatures had lived on Earth for so long before humans even arrived.

We walked around, looking at the exhibits and reading the signs. "Ooh, look," Daphne said. "There's a flying reptile, like the pterodactyls Dr. Sharkey was talking about."

"That's a small one," said Professor Peabody. "Its wingspan is about three feet. Some of the later pterodactyls had wingspans of up to forty feet!"

"Jinkies!" I said, trying to imagine a flying reptile that huge. It could probably pick up something as big as an elephant or a truck and carry it away. Maybe it was a good thing that they were extinct!

"Here's one of our most recent acquisitions," the professor said, pointing to a large skeleton mounted in the middle of the room.

"This is a stegosaurus that was found right here in the United States."

"In Texas," added a tall man in a cowboy hat. He wore red leather cowboy boots and a denim jacket. He was standing on the other side of the dinosaur. "On my ranch, to be exact."

"Mr. Walker, what a surprise," said the professor, who didn't sound surprised at all. "Kids, this is Mr. Walker. He has been a frequent visitor to the museum lately."

Mr. Walker tipped his hat. "Pleased to meet you," he drawled. "And I'm extremely pleased to have you meet Dinah."

Fred looked around. We were the only people in the room. "Who's Dinah?" he asked.

Mr. Walker nodded toward the stegosaurus skeleton. "Why, that's Dinah. Dinah the dinosaur. I got to know her real well when I was helping to dig her up. She's a beauty, ain't she?"

"She sure is," Daphne said. "Is she from the Jurassic period, too?"

"Heck, I don't know," shrugged Mr. Walker. "All I know is that she turned up on my land. I found her when I was digging for oil. That means I oughta get some of the credit — and some of the money. She's worth a pretty penny, I can tell you."

The professor sighed. "She is valuable," he admitted. "But mostly as a scientific specimen. As I've told you, Mr. Walker, the museum cannot afford to pay you anything for this dinosaur. She may have been found on your land, but she belongs to science now."

"We'll see about that," said Mr. Walker, tipping his hat and grinning at us before he turned and walked out the door.

Fred's Mystery-Solving Tips

"Dinosaurs sure are fascinating. I could spend all day at this museum! There's so much to learn. But we have a mystery to solve, too. Did you notice 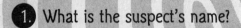 in this entry? That means you've met another suspect. Try to answer the following questions, and you'll be on your way to solving this dino-mystery!"

1. What is the suspect's name?

2. What does the suspect do for a living?

3. Why would the suspect steal the pterodactyl eggs?

"Good work! Now, let's go check out the rest of the museum."

15

Clue-Keeper Entry 3

Professor Peabody shook his head as he watched Mr. Walker stroll away. "I wish I could make him understand," he said. Then he brightened. "Oh, well. Why don't we continue our tour? Anything else you'd like to see? We have lots of other things here besides dinosaurs."

"Like, I don't know about anybody else,"

16

Shaggy said, "but I'd like to see a hamburger and some fries. I'm starving!"

"*Re, roo!*" Scooby agreed.

The professor laughed. "Well, we wouldn't want you to go hungry. There's a snack bar in the museum. We can head there as soon as we finish our tour. First I'd like to show you the rest of the museum. How does that sound?"

"Groovy," Shaggy said.

"*Rrroovy*," Scooby added.

"What's in the next room?" Fred asked, pointing toward a doorway.

"That's the Hall of Mammals," the professor said. "We have dioramas featuring everything from the smallest mouse to the largest whale, all shown in their natural habitats. I think you'll enjoy it."

We walked through the doorway and into another large hall filled with glass cases. Hanging in the center of this hall was a model of a gigantic blue whale.

"Wow!" I said, staring up at it. "That's beautiful." I could just imagine it swimming through the ocean. It was amazing to think about this creature, almost as big as the biggest dinosaurs, but still living on earth.

We walked around the room, looking at all the dioramas. There was one featuring woodland animals like deer, raccoons, and foxes. Another showed an Arctic scene, with a polar bear and some beautiful seals.

"Look at the lion!" Daphne said, pointing at the diorama that showed animal life on the plains of Africa. "And the giraffes and ostriches. Cool!"

"If you like that sort of thing," sniffed a short, red-haired woman standing next to us. She was wearing a navy blue suit and high heels. "In my museum, the displays are much more lifelike. And we use computers to show the information instead of relying on these old-fashioned signs."

"Are you a museum director?" I asked, looking around for Professor Peabody. I was hoping he wouldn't get his feelings hurt by overhearing this woman insult his displays. Fortunately, he was on the other side of the room, showing Fred, Shaggy, and Scooby the display of otters.

"Yes, I am. My name's Ms. Murgatroyd, and I run the Steam City Museum of Natural History. It's a wonderful place. You should visit!"

"Maybe sometime," Daphne said. "If you don't mind my asking, why are you here if you think this museum is so old-fashioned?"

Ms. Murgatroyd looked around. Then she leaned forward and whispered. "Just between you and me, I'm on a mission," she said. "I'm hoping to convince Professor Peabody that this museum isn't worth keeping open anymore. If I do, he'll sell me some of his specimens. That T-Rex for example — it's an excellent skeleton. But it's wasted here. Nobody sees it. We could give it an excellent home in Steam City!" She smiled at us.

Just then, Professor Peabody walked over, followed by the guys and Scooby. "Well, hello there, Ms. Murgatroyd," he said, forcing a smile. "How lovely to see you again."

"Have you changed your mind yet?" she asked him.

"Never," he answered, folding his arms. "I told you I'll never change my mind. This museum will stay open no matter what!"

"This museum is the best. I can see why Professor Peabody wants to keep it open! I sure hope he can. If we can solve this mystery, maybe that will help. And we're getting closer all the time. Did you notice the 👁️👁️ in this entry? That means we've found another suspect. See if you can answer the following questions."

1. What is the suspect's name?

2. What does the suspect do for a living?

3. Why would the suspect steal the pterodactyl eggs?

Clue-Keeper Entry 4

"Well," said Professor Peabody, after we'd said good-bye to Ms. Murgatroyd. "How about that hamburger you mentioned? I could go for some fries myself."

"All right!" Shaggy and Scooby said together, nodding eagerly.

"I think you'll enjoy our snack bar," said the Professor as he led us down a hall, around a corner, and back through the Great Hall. He brought us past the diplodoccus and down another hallway, pointing out the gift shop as we went by. Finally, he threw open some big double doors. We all gasped.

Suddenly, it was as if we were in a tropical jungle. Plants and trees filled the room, which was lit from above by a giant skylight. Water burbled in streams and fountains, and there was a large pond in the middle of the room, filled with huge goldfish.

"Jinkies!" I said. "This is wonderful!"

"And the skylight even opens on nice days, to let in sun and air," the professor said proudly. "This atrium is one of the museum's best features."

We walked around the room, gasping at the beautiful flowers that covered vines hanging from the trees. "This is just beautiful," Daphne said.

"Like, sure, it's beautiful," Shaggy agreed. "But, like, where are the burgers?"

The professor laughed. "Just beyond this palm tree here," he said, continuing to lead the way.

"Phew," Shaggy said when we walked up to the snack bar. "Just in time. I'm so hungry I could eat a diplodocus." He looked over the menu that was posted behind the counter. "Let's see, do I want the extra large Mastodon Burger or the Mesozoic Chili Dog?" He looked at Scooby. "Are you thinking what I'm thinking?" he asked.

Scooby nodded.

"Two of each," Shaggy told the woman behind the counter.

"Two of each *what*?" she asked.

"Two of each of everything on the menu," Shaggy answered happily.

The girl blinked. Then she smiled. "Coming right up," she said.

The rest of us put in our orders, too, and we sat down at a table to wait. Mr. Walker and Ms. Murgatroyd sat at a table nearby, and I spotted Dr. Sharkey standing near the snack bar, putting in an order. "Your museum is wonderful," I told Professor Peabody, "with or without the pterodactyl eggs."

"Thank you," he sighed. "But if attendance doesn't go up soon, we may have to close."

Just then I looked up and saw a shadow move across the skylight. "Do you have birds in here?" I asked.

"Birds?" the professor asked. "No. Why do you ask?"

"I just thought I saw something flying

around," I answered. "Hey! There it is again!"

This time, the shadow swooped closer, and what I saw made a chill go down my spine. "It's — it's —" I began.

"It can't be," gasped the professor. He leaped to his feet.

"What is it?" Daphne asked.

"It's a pterodactyl," the professor answered. "It can't be, but it is."

The shadow swooped closer and closer, and soon we could all see that it was a gigantic flying reptile. As it flew toward us, it suddenly let out an earsplitting shriek.

"Help!" yelled Shaggy.

"That thing is huge!" said Fred. "The wingspan must be eight feet!" He ducked as the pterodactyl swooped down, claws outstretched.

"I'm getting out of here!" Shaggy said, dashing for the door.

"*Rait ror re!*" yelled Scooby, running after him.

"We're right behind you," I said. Daphne, Fred, the professor, and I all rushed toward the door. The pterodactyl swooped and shrieked, chasing us through the trees.

Ms. Murgatroyd and Mr. Walker jumped up from the table and ran, too. "Don't panic!" yelled Mr. Walker, in a panicky voice.

We slipped through the door just in time. "Whew!" said Fred. "I could practically feel his claws grabbing on to me."

Ms. Murgatroyd was comforting Mr.

Walker over in the corner. "Take deep breaths," she said.

Dr. Sharkey came out of the door last. His hair was as disheveled as always, and he looked distracted. He headed off down the hall without saying a word to anyone.

The professor stood there, panting. His face was white. "This can't be happening," he said. "It must be an illusion. A robot, or a holograph. Pterodactyls have been extinct for thousands of years."

"I wonder," I said, thinking out loud. "Maybe somebody created this pretend pterodactyl to try to scare us away before we figure out the mystery of the missing eggs."

"Nobody can scare us away," Daphne said. "Not when we're on the case."

"Speak for yourself," Shaggy told her.

"Don't listen to him," Fred told Professor Peabody. "Daphne's right. We'll get to the bottom of this mystery. Don't worry."

"Let's split up and look for clues," I suggested. "Shaggy and Scooby can check out this area of the museum. Daphne and Fred

and I will go see what we can find on the other side of the Great Hall. Then we can meet back here and compare notes."

"Good plan," said Fred.

"Thank you, thank you," said the professor, wringing his hands. "I certainly hope you can help!"

"We promise to do our best," I said.

Clue-Keeper Entry 5

Before we split up, I looked over at Ms. Murgatroyd to see how she and Mr. Walker were doing. "Are you two okay?" I asked.

"Oh, sure," said Ms. Murgatroyd. "Wasn't that amazing? I felt as if I were back in the Mesozoic era, with a pterodactyl flying over my head."

Mr. Walked stared at her. "You enjoyed that?" he asked.

"Well, not exactly. I was scared, too," she admitted. "But there was something exciting about it."

"Give me a good old bucking bronco anytime," said Mr. Walker. "That's my type of excitement."

"Hmmm, bucking broncos or pterodactyls," Shaggy said, as if he were trying to decide which was more exciting. "Like, who needs that kind of excitement?"

"Not me," Daphne said. "That pterodactyl was terrifying. What are you going to do about it, Professor Peabody?"

"Well, first of all, I guess the snack bar is closed for business for now," he said.

"Noooo!" moaned Shaggy. Scooby groaned.

He ignored them. "And then, well, I guess we'll just have to wait and see. If we can solve the mystery of the missing eggs, maybe we can figure out who created the pretend pterodactyl." Professor Peabody looked around at us. "Anyway, the main thing is that we're all safe."

"I almost didn't escape," said Mr. Walker, who still looked scared. "I nearly tripped and fell while I was cutting through the red-flowered vines in that crazy tropical rain forest in there." He held up a chunk of rock. "I grabbed this so nobody else would have the same problem."

"What is that?" asked Ms. Murgatroyd, peering at the object.

"Whatever it is, I can't imagine what it's doing in the atrium," said Professor Peabody. "That garden is perfectly landscaped. Nothing changes in there without my knowledge." He leaned in to look at the rock.

"Can we see?" I asked. I stepped forward to take a look. So did the rest of the gang. The object was tan and had an interesting leathery look.

"Like, big deal," Shaggy said. "It's just a rock."

"I'm not so sure about that," said Ms. Murgatroyd. "I have a feeling this may be much more than just an ordinary rock."

Professor Peabody stared at her. "You don't think—" he began.

"Yes, I do," said Ms. Murgatroyd. "I think that this may be a piece of shell from one of those missing pterodactyl eggs."

Mr. Walker burst out laughing. "Now, that's a tall tale if I ever heard one," he said, slapping his knee. "Good joke!"

"I don't think she's joking," Fred said. "I think Ms. Murgatroyd might be right. It looks just like Dr. Sharkey's description."

"Oh, my," said Professor Peabody. "Could this mean —" His face was white.

"— that the pterodactyl is real, after all?" Ms. Murgatroyd finished. She looked excited. "Maybe it could! Maybe it somehow hatched from this egg!"

"That's just silly," Mr. Walker said. "Why, that thing looks more like one of them ostrich eggs I saw in a case than anything else."

Professor Peabody ignored him. "It does seem highly unlikely, from a scientific standpoint," he said. "But why don't I give it to Dr. Sharkey? Perhaps he can run some tests on it."

He took the object and hurried off down the hall.

Mr. Walker and Ms. Murgatroyd headed off, talking about the mysterious object. Her high heels *click-click-clicked* as they disappeared around a corner. The rest of us split up to look for more clues. "You be careful," I told Shaggy and Scooby.

"Of course we will," Shaggy said. "But, like, you don't have to worry. What could possibly go wrong?"

"Jinkies! Things are getting mighty strange around here. This museum is full of surprises. Did you catch the clue in the last entry? If you saw the , you can probably answer these questions."

1. What clue did you find in this entry?

2. Which of the suspects might be responsible for the clue?

3. What does this clue tell you about the missing eggs?

"Good work! All we need is another clue or two, and we'll be on our way to solving this prehistoric puzzle."

Clue-Keeper Entry 6

"So," Shaggy said to Scooby, "time to look for clues. Any ideas?"

Scooby just shrugged. "*Ruh-ruh,*" he said, shaking his head. (Shaggy told me all this later, when we met again.)

"Why don't we go talk to Dr. Sharkey?" Shaggy suggested. "Maybe he's learned something about that egg."

"*Rokay*," Scooby said.

The two of them headed down the quiet hallway until they came to a doorway marked CURATOR.

"This must be it," Shaggy said. He knocked on the door.

"Go away!" yelled someone from inside.

"Dr. Sharkey?" Shaggy called.

There was a pause. "He's not here," said the voice.

"Like, that sounds exactly like Dr. Sharkey," Shaggy said, confused. He knocked again.

"Go away! I'm busy!"

Shaggy and Scooby exchanged a look and a shrug. "I guess we're not going to talk to Dr. Sharkey right now. Any other ideas?"

Scooby looked thoughtful. Then his stomach gave a loud rumble.

"Hungry?" Shaggy asked.

Scooby nodded hard.

"Me, too," Shaggy said. "Tell you what. Let's go back to the snack bar and get all the food we ordered. It's probably all sitting there, waiting for us."

Scooby's eyes grew wide. He shook his head. "*Ro ray*," he said.

"It's okay," Shaggy said. "We'll be really, really quiet. Like, the pterodactyl won't even know we're there. We'll tiptoe in, grab the food, and leave. Come on, Scooby, I'm as scared of that thing as you are. But I'm starving!"

Scooby finally agreed, and they headed back to the atrium. Shaggy eased the door open very, very quietly, and they slipped

inside. They went right to the snack bar and saw that there was nobody behind the counter. But the counter itself was piled high with food: hamburgers, fries, hot dogs, pizza, nachos, and chips, everything Scooby and Shaggy had ordered.

They scooped as much food as they could into their arms and started to slink away. Just then, there was a flapping noise right above them. "Run!" shouted Shaggy. "We can hide in those bushes."

They took off, leaving a trail of french fries, and headed for a clump of trees. The pterodactyl swooped behind them, screeching loudly.

"Duck in here!" said Shaggy, holding aside a vine covered with red flowers. Scooby ducked.

"Phew," said Shaggy. "I think we're safe." He grinned at Scooby. "And we even have most of our food!"

Scooby glared at him.

"Okay, okay," Shaggy said. "Like, I know you told me so. But it'll turn out okay. We can hunker down in here as long as we want, now that we have provisions." He took a huge bite of a hamburger.

Scooby pointed to something on the ground.

"What's that, buddy?" Shaggy asked. He took a closer look. "Hey, it's some more of that egg thing. This must be where Mr. Walker tripped." He looked around. "Yup, sure enough. There are his footprints. I can tell those were made by cowboy boots. And here are some other footprints. They look like . . . sneakers!"

Scooby nodded.

"Cool," Shaggy said. "Man, this mystery-solving stuff is hard work. I'm ready for another burger. How about you?"

Scooby held out a paw and grinned.

Shaggy and Scooby's
Mystery-Solving Tips

"Like, so, maybe it wasn't so smart to go back into the atrium. That huge bird-thing almost got us! But we made it to safety. And, like, I think we even found a clue! Did you see the ○━━▷? Cool. Then answer these questions."

1. What clue did you find in this entry?

2. Which suspect might be responsible for the clue?

3. Can you eliminate any suspects with this clue?

"Great! While you answer the questions, Scooby and I will finish our snack. Then we'll figure out how we're going to get out of this place without the pterodactyl seeing us!"

44

Clue-Keeper Entry 7

While Scooby and Shaggy were huddling in the atrium, the rest of us were checking out other parts of the museum.

"Where should we start?" Fred asked.

"Let's go to the Great Hall," Daphne suggested. "From there we can go through every other room and make sure we don't miss anything."

Back in the Great Hall, we gazed up at the diplodocus. "I wish you could help us, old pal," joked Fred, talking to the gigantic skull.

"He can't, but Dinah might be able to," said Mr. Walker, who was strolling past. He winked at us. "That Dinah's a mighty smart dinosaur."

I knew he was just kidding, but I figured we might as well check out the dinosaur room next. We had to look everywhere for clues.

I stared into each of the cases on one side of the room, looking everything over carefully. Fred and Daphne were on the other side. We met at the end of the room. "Anything?" I asked.

"Nothing," Daphne said, shaking her head.

"Maybe Mr. Walker's right," Fred said. "Maybe we should ask Dinah." He walked over to the big stegosaurus skeleton in the middle of the room. "Dinah," he said. "Where can we find a clue?"

But Dinah didn't answer. I guess that was a good thing. After that pterodactyl, I

wasn't sure I wanted any other dinosaurs to come to life!

"Hmm," I said. "If I had stolen pterodactyl eggs, where would I hide them? It would be dangerous to try to get them out of the museum, since a guard might see you. So maybe you'd hide them *in* the museum."

"Good thinking," said Fred. "But they'd have to be in a place nobody would think to look."

"For example, in one of these displays!" said Daphne. "I mean, what if you hid the eggs in plain sight? Wouldn't that be clever?"

We stared at each other.

Suddenly, I remembered what Mr. Walker had said about the eggs looking like ostrich eggs. "This way!" I said. "Follow me!" I dashed into the Hall of Mammals and headed straight for the Africa diorama. There, behind a locked glass case, was a nest of ostrich eggs.

But two of the eggs looked just a *little* different from the others! They were a little

larger, a little darker, and a little more leathery.

"Look," I said, pointing. "I bet those are the pterodactyl eggs!"

"I think you're right," Fred said. "Professor Peabody is going to be so happy!"

"There's still a problem, though," I said. "We don't know who stole them."

"And there's one other thing," said Daphne. "That pterodactyl is still in the atrium. And it probably will be, until we figure out who our thief is."

"**W**ow! We found the eggs! Now if we can just solve the rest of the mystery, maybe Professor Peabody's museum will be able to stay open after all. I bet you noticed the 🔦 in the last entry. That means you found another clue! Can you answer these questions?"

1. What clue did you find in this entry?

2. Which suspect might be responsible for the clue?

3. How do you know?

"Good work. We've almost got this mystery solved!"

50

Clue-Keeper Entry 8

Fred, Daphne, and I went back toward the atrium. We found Scooby and Shaggy standing just outside the doors. Each of them was balancing a gigantic leaf on his head.

"What are you two doing?" asked Daphne, giggling. "You look very silly!"

"Silly, maybe. But we're alive!" Shaggy said. "We used these leaves as a disguise to help us sneak away from the pterodactyl. Like, it didn't even see us leaving. It's still flying around in there, yelling its head off." He explained how they'd gotten caught in the atrium when they went in to find food.

"Oh, Shaggy," I said. "If you and Scooby could just forget about food, you'd stay out of trouble."

Scooby hung his head. Then he licked a spot of ketchup off his chin. "*Rood ries!*" he said.

"That's right, Scooby," said Shaggy. "They were good fries. Worth a little trouble. Plus, we found a clue!" He told us about the footprints.

"Hmm," said Fred. "I'm beginning to think we can solve this case. All we need to do is catch that pterodactyl and find out where it came from."

"That sounds hard," said Shaggy.

"Not really," said Fred. "Not if we use my plan. Since you two like disguises so much, why don't you put these on?" He held up two dinosaur costumes. "I got these from the gift shop. If you and Scooby put them on and go into the atrium, the pterodactyl will come down to check you out. Then we'll set off a smoke bomb. Without any visibility, the pterodactyl won't be able to take off again, and we can catch it."

Shaggy just stared at us.

I turned to Scooby. "How about it, Scooby?"

"*Ro ray,*" he said, shaking his head.

Daphne took over. "Would you do it for two Scooby Snacks and an order of fries?"

Scooby thought for a second. "*Rokay!*" he

said, taking the costume from Fred and pulling it on. Daphne and I threw him the snacks, and he gobbled them up. Then he turned to Shaggy and raised his eyebrows.

"Oh, okay," Shaggy said, sighing. He put on his costume. Then he and Scooby opened the door to the atrium and slipped inside. We peeked through the door to watch.

There was a loud screech as the pterodactyl spotted them and swooped down.

"Now!" yelled Daphne, and Fred tossed in the smoke bomb. Immediately, the entire atrium was filled with smoke.

Just then, Professor Peabody came along. "What's this?" he asked, peering into the atrium. "Why, I can't see a thing in there. Better open the skylight to let that smoke out." He flipped a big switch.

The huge skylight slid open and smoke poured out. As soon as it could see, the pterodactyl took off, holding Shaggy in one huge talon and Scooby in the other.

"Help!" yelled Shaggy.

"Relp!" shouted Scooby.

The pterodactyl flapped as hard as it could, but it was carrying too much weight. Finally, it had to let go, and Shaggy and Scooby plummeted into a large palm tree.

Without the weight, the pterodactyl had no trouble flying higher. It circled up, up, up and then disappeared out of the skylight.

"Ruh-roh," we all heard Scooby say from his perch in the palm tree. But somebody else seemed even more upset. "NO! NO! Come back! Don't go!" Loud sobs filled the air.

There was still too much smoke in the atrium for us to be able to see who was shouting and sobbing.

"I think I hear a thief," said Fred. "Whoever's crying must be the one who stole the eggs and created the pterodactyl. Let's go see who it is."

"**Y**ikes!" you say. "What an exciting mystery." It's a little scary to think about the idea that a pterodactyl might still be out there, flying around. But you're glad the gang figured out who stole the eggs.

"It was a tough one," Fred says. "But we solved it. How about you? Do you think you know who the thief was?"

"Think about it," Velma says. "Look over my notes in the Clue Keeper, and think about each of the suspects you met. Which of them has the best reason for stealing the eggs?"

"Now think about the clues you found," adds Daphne. "Which of the suspects might have left those clues?"

"Try to eliminate any suspects who could *not* have left the clues," Fred says. "That might help."

"And have another scoop of ice cream," Shaggy suggests helpfully. "I always do my best thinking on a full stomach." He jumps up to go to the counter. "I'll get you one if you want. What flavor?"

"Nothing for now, Shaggy," you say. You need to concentrate if you're going to solve this mystery.

"Go ahead and check all your notes," says Daphne. "Then, when you're ready, we'll tell you who the thief was."

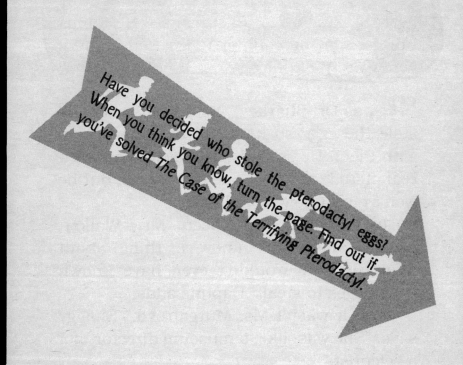

Have you decided who stole the pterodactyl eggs? When you think you know, turn the page. Find out if you've solved The Case of the Terrifying Pterodactyl.

"It was Dr. Sharkey!" Velma tells you. "He stole the eggs so he could do experiments with them. He actually managed to create a real pterodactyl from one of the eggs, but he won't reveal how he did it."

"It couldn't have been Mr. Walker, because he didn't know a thing about dinosaurs. He wouldn't even have known which eggs to steal!" Daphne adds.

"And it wasn't Ms. Murgatroyd," Shaggy says. "She was, like, a museum director, not a scientist."

"We figured out it had to be Dr. Sharkey

because he was a scientist, and the only person who had the keys to open the diorama with the ostrich eggs," Fred says.

"The professor must have been happy to have the case solved," you say.

"He was," says Daphne. "But now his curator is going to jail. I think he may ask Ms. Murgatroyd to come run the museum with him."

"What about the pterodactyl?" you ask.

Fred shrugs. "Professor Peabody thinks it

probably found its way to the deepest, darkest jungle it could find, away from any humans. There's no way we could find it again, so we'll just let it live its life in peace."

"Wow," you say. "That's some story. You all worked hard to solve that mystery."

"Like, that's no joke," Shaggy says. "And I worked up an appetite, too. How about it, Scooby? Are you ready to try all the flavors we missed last time around?"

"Rooby-rooby-roo!" says Scooby, with a huge grin.